ANIMALS

Please return / renew by date shown.
You can renew it at:
norlink.norfolk.gov.uk
or by telephone: 0344 800 8006
Please have your library card & PIN ready

NORFOLK LIBRARY
AND INFORMATION SERVICE

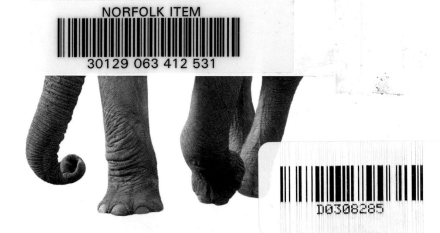

ANIMALS ON THE EDGE ELEPHANT

by Anna Claybourne

BLOOMSBURY

LONDON BERLIN NEW YORK SYDNEY

Published 2012 by
Bloomsbury Publishing Plc
50 Bedford Square, London, WC1B 3DP

www.bloomsbury.com

ISBN HB 978-1-4081-4827-3
ISBN PB 978-1-4081-4958-4

Picture acknowledgements:
Cover: Shutterstock
Insides: All Shutterstock except for the following; p7 bottom left ©Thomas Breuer via Wikimedia Commons, p14 bottom right ©ZSL, p15 top ©ZSL, p15 ©William Gordon Davis/ZSL, p18 ©James Godwin/ZSL, p19 centre left ©James Godwin/ZSL, p19 top and centre right ©ZSL, p21 centre left ©Hannah Thompson/ZSL, p21 centre right ©ZSL, p23 both images ©ZSL, p27 top inset ©ZSL, p30 bottom ©ZSL/ECN, p31 both images ©ZSL/ECN, p34 bottom left ©ZSL/ECN, p35 middle left ©ZSL/ECN, p39 all images ©ZSL, p41 bottom right ©Hannah Thompson/ZSL

Manufactured and supplied under licence from the Zoological Society of London.

Produced for Bloomsbury Publishing Plc by Geoff Ward.

A CIP catalogue for this book is available from the British Library.

Printed in China by C&C Offset Printing Co.

FSC
www.fsc.org

MIX
Paper from
responsible sources
FSC® C008047

CONTENTS

MEET THE ELEPHANT

There's no mistaking an elephant. With its long, twisting trunk and giant flapping ears, it looks like no other creature in the world. And of course, it's also the biggest animal that lives on land.

How big?

REALLY big! A large **bull** (male) African elephant can be 7m long and almost 4m tall – bigger than most classrooms. He has a trunk and tusks up to 2m long – more than a man's height – and ears the size of a double bed. If you put him on a giant set of weighing scales, you'd have to put 200 ten-year-olds on the other side to make it balance!

DID YOU KNOW?

- Elephants cannot jump
- An elephant can run at 40km/h – faster than most humans
- There are 40,000 muscles in an elephant's trunk
- Elephants are good swimmers
- Elephants can sleep standing up

The **African savannah elephant** is the biggest elephant. It lives in grasslands, forests, **scrub** and farmland across most of Africa.

What are elephants like?

Elephants are plant-eaters, and mostly live in small groups. They are very strong and intelligent. They are found in Africa and Asia, and there are two different **species**, and one elephant **subspecies** or type.

Elephants in trouble

There aren't nearly as many elephants as there used to be. Experts think that about 500,000 African savannah elephants live in the wild, and their numbers have now started to go up again. But Asian elephants are much more **rare**. There may be only about 30,000 of them left. There is a lot of **conservation** work going on to help elephants survive. You can read more about it later in this book.

The **Asian elephant** has a rounder head and smaller ears than African elephants, and females don't have tusks. It lives mainly in forests in south-east Asia, from India to Indonesia.

The **African forest elephant** is closely related to the African savannah elephant. It lives in the forests of Central and West Africa.

FACT FILE: LATIN NAMES

Like all living things, each elephant species has its own special scientific name, written in Latin.

African elephant	*Loxodonta africana*
Forest elephant	*Loxodonta cyclotis*
Asian elephant	*Elephas maximus*

African savannah elephant   Human

ELEPHANTS ON THE EDGE

Like many wild animals, elephants are in trouble – and it's mainly because of human activities. Sadly, people have hunted and harmed millions of elephants.

Problems for elephants

There are usually lots of reasons why a species becomes rare and at risk. This is especially true with elephants. They have been hunted for sport, for their skin and meat – and most of all, for their tusks, which are used as **ivory**. They are killed to protect farms and villages from them. In the past, a lot of elephants were also captured to be used as working animals. Elephants have also suffered from **habitat loss**. This happens when people take over their **habitats** – the wild places where they live – to make farmland, roads or towns.

Endangered species

An organisation called the **IUCN**, short for International Union for Conservation of Nature, keeps lists of animals that are in danger of **extinction** in the wild. The Asian elephant is listed as **endangered**. This means it is at risk of dying out.

African elephants are listed as **vulnerable**, which is almost as serious as "endangered". Experts aren't sure how many African forest elephants there are left – but they think they are endangered too.

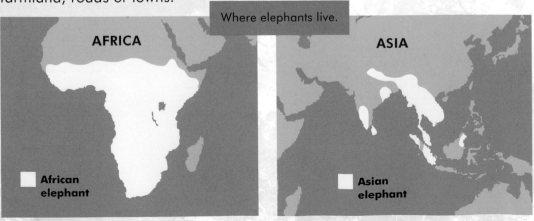

Where elephants live.

AFRICA

ASIA

African elephant

Asian elephant

Edge of existence

The Asian elephant is also listed by the **EDGE** of Existence programme as an EDGE species. That means it is not only endangered, but unusual and has few relatives. If animals like this die out, there will be nothing like them left. **ZSL**, the Zoological Society of London, runs the EDGE programme and is working on conservation projects to help the Asian elephant.

THE ASIAN ELEPHANT

Why is the Asian elephant more at risk? One big reason is that Asian countries often have bigger human **populations** than African countries. Lots more people live there, and they need more space for farmland and homes. So elephants have only been left with small patches of wild land here and there.

A road now cuts through the forest in Thailand where these Asian elephants live.

THE ELEPHANT'S COUSINS

Elephants aren't closely related to other large land animals, like hippos and rhinos. Instead, their closest relatives are water animals called manatees and dugongs, and the hyrax, a much smaller animal. Other types of elephants, such as the woolly mammoth, are now extinct.

Hyraxes look more like guinea pigs than elephants, but they are elephants' closest living relatives.

ELEPHANTS IN THE WILD

In the wild, you won't usually see just one elephant, but a herd. Elephants are **very** sociable – especially female elephants. They like to live in groups and look after each other.

Family groups

An elephant herd is made up of about 10 elephants. They are all either adult **cows** (females), or **calves** (babies). The leader is usually an older female, called the **matriarch**. The others in the herd are her own babies, her grown-up daughters, and *their* babies. So the matriarch is really a grandma who is in charge of the family. Male elephants can live alone, or get together in small groups.

Elephants keep growing as they get older, so the old matriarch or grandma is usually the biggest in the herd.

LONG-DISTANCE CALLS

Elephants can tell what's happening a long way away, by detecting **vibrations** that travel through the ground. They can sense a thunderstorm that will bring rain, a **stampede** of animals that might mean danger, or low, rumbling noises made by other elephants.

Safety in numbers

Adult elephants are too big for other animals to hunt, but lions do sometimes hunt elephant calves. So all the elephants in the herd help to protect the babies. At night, or if there's a **predator** around, the adults form a circle around the calves, to keep them safe.

On the move

Elephants need to eat for most of the day. They have a large home **range**, or area, and wander around it to find food and water. An elephant herd can spend 16 hours each day moving around and feeding. In that time, they can walk up to 80km. However, they never wander too far from a river or **watering hole**, as they need a nice big drink of water at least once a day.

An elephant's trunk has many uses. It's so strong it can pick up a huge log, yet the tip is so delicate, it can pick up a peanut!

Elephants love spraying themselves with water to cool down, and rolling in mud to protect their skin from sunburn and insect bites.

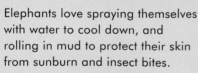

THE AMAZING TRUNK

An elephant's trunk is incredibly useful. Elephants use their trunks to:

- Suck up water to drink
- Suck up water to shower with
- Breathe through, and use as a snorkel when underwater
- Smell food, danger, and other elephants
- Make a loud trumpeting sound
- Push things over
- Pick up heavy objects
- Pick up small objects using the finger-like tip of the trunk
- Cuddle, stroke or hold on to other elephants
- To reach for food that is high up like mangos
- To pull down food like branches and bamboo

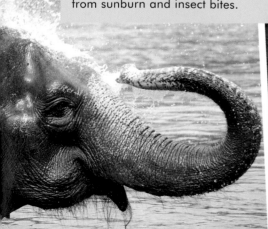

ELEPHANTS AND US

Since ancient times, especially in India and Thailand, humans have kept elephants as pets, trained them to do useful jobs, and even worshipped them as holy animals.

Working elephants

As the elephant is so big and powerful, it used to be seen as a suitable animal for a king. Famous rulers might ride an elephant in a royal ceremony or procession, or even into battle. Elephants can do other, less glamorous work too, such as **logging**. Instead of people cutting down trees, they can train elephants to push them over and carry the logs to where they are needed.

Elephants dressed in golden decorations take part in a festival in Kerala, India.

A brain for learning

Elephants are clever. They can learn how to follow lots of different instructions, using different commands and signals. Traditionally, elephants were trained from a young age, and each elephant had its own trainer and keeper, called a **mahout**. This still happens, to train elephants for forest work, or for riding, but it's much less common than it used to be.

ELEPHANTS AT WAR

Elephants were used as war animals for thousands of years. Most working elephants are female, but males were used in war because they are more **aggressive**. War elephants looked scary, could charge and trample enemy armies, and give their riders a safe height and a good view.

Is it cruel?

Some of the methods used to train elephants can be cruel, and some working elephants get injured and worn out. There are elephant rescue centres for working elephants that have been mistreated, and campaigns against cruel training methods. However, elephants can also learn by being given rewards, instead of being treated harshly.

Many cultures have elephant gods, legends or beliefs. This is Ganesha, the elephant-headed god of new beginnings, in the Hindu religion.

DO ELEPHANTS EVER FORGET?

A famous saying about elephants claims, "Elephants never forget!" and it seems there really is some truth in it. Elephants can often recognise other elephants or zookeepers when they meet them, even after years apart. Wild elephants also seem to remember when humans have harmed them. Their ability to learn also shows that they have a good memory.

A working elephant carrying branches, with its trainer riding on top.

ELEPHANTS IN ZOOS

Around the world, there are about 2,000 elephants living in zoos. They are very popular with visitors.

What do elephants need?

Elephants need space, so their zoo **enclosures** have to be big. They also like natural surroundings like grass, pools to bathe in, and trees and rocks to rub against. Although elephants come from Africa and Asia, they don't mind cool temperatures – but they do need an indoor area where they can shelter from storms, or enjoy some privacy if they want to.

Booooored!

As elephants are intelligent, they can get bored. Zoos have to provide ways to keep them interested and entertained. They hide food for the elephants to find, and give them wooden poles to push and scratch against. Some elephants enjoy playing with toys, like swinging tyres or bouncy balls.

A baby elephant at ZSL Whipsnade Zoo gets to grips with a rubber tyre.

Elephants are very strong, so their enclosures need super-strong fences or walls that they can't break through.

ZSL Whipsnade Zoo's herd of Asian elephants go for a walk, holding onto each other tightly!

Jumbo carried several people at a time on his back.

Who's in the zoo?

All three species of elephants can live in zoos. But Asian elephants are the most common, as they're smaller and easier to look after. Also, as they are endangered, zoos keep them to study them and try to help them survive.

Emotional elephants

Elephants are happier if they can be close to other elephants. Most zoos try to recreate a natural elephant herd, so that female elephants can be with their family members, and spend time together. Male elephants are harder to look after, as they sometimes enter a bad-tempered, violent state called **musth**, when they can be very dangerous.

JUMBO

Jumbo, an African bull elephant, was one of the best-known zoo elephants ever. He was born in Sudan, Africa, and taken to a zoo in Paris, then to London Zoo in 1865. He was very popular with visitors, and famous for giving children rides. The name Jumbo came from the African word "Jambo" meaning "hello". Because of Jumbo the elephant, the word "jumbo" is now used to mean "enormous".

WHAT ELEPHANTS EAT

Elephants eat plants. Which plants, and which parts of them, depends on the elephant and where it lives. Whatever they eat, elephants need a massive amount of it every day.

How much?

An adult elephant gobbles up between 150 and 300kg of plant based food per day, the same weight as about 1,000 apples! African savannah elephants eat more grasses and leaves, while Asian and forest elephants find more fruit. But all elephants can eat grass, leaves, roots, fruits, plant stalks, **shoots**, nuts, seeds, and even tree bark. On top of that, an elephant drinks up to 250 litres of water each day, enough to fill a bathtub right to the top.

In the zoo

In the zoo, keepers feed the elephants on hay, leafy branches called **browse**, and fruit and veg such as bananas, apples, pears, cabbage and carrots. They also have **herbivore pellets**, a special food designed for plant-eaters.

As elephants eat for most of the day, they need food all the time. To make it more exciting for them, the keepers spread the food around different parts of the enclosure for them to find. Sometimes they put it on high platforms, or hide it in special feeders that have lots of holes and cracks for the elephants to reach their trunks into.

A zoo elephant reaches up to collect a mouthful of hay from a dangling hay feeder.

Elephant buns

In old songs and stories, zoo elephants eat buns and cakes. Long ago this was true – visitors could buy buns and feed them to the elephants. Today, they don't have buns very often, because they are bad for their teeth. But elephants still love buns, so they might get one on their birthday or at Christmas!

To drink, elephants suck water into their trunks, then squirt it into their mouths.

ELEPHANT FOOD SHOPPING LIST

At most zoos, the elephant food shopping list looks like this:

Hay
Carrots
Oranges
Pears
Herbivore pellets

Bananas
Cabbages
Apples
Maize
Fruit tree branches

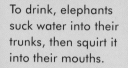

ELEPHANT POO

After eating so much food, a typical elephant makes a LOT of poo, or **dung** – enough to fill a big wheelbarrow each day. In the wild, it's a useful **fertilizer**, making the soil better for plants to grow in. It also provides food for some animals, such as the dung beetle.

This African elephant has picked up a big, tasty branch to munch on.

A DAY IN THE LIFE: ELEPHANT KEEPER

Elizabeth Becker is one of the elephant keepers at ZSL Whipsnade Zoo. She reveals what it's like working with elephants, and all the jobs that have to be done.

A day with the elephants

7:30am The first job of the day is to check the elephants are all OK, and give them their breakfast. While they're eating, we clean out their sleeping quarters.

8:30am Each elephant gets a bath and a scrub down using warm water and shampoo. We take this chance to check they're healthy, as well as clean! After this we let them out into the paddocks.

10.00am Time for one-to-one training for the younger elephants. Using a reward-based approach (that is, plenty of bananas!) we train our elephants to obey commands, such as lie down, go in a certain direction, and most important of all, STOP! This is essential for working safely with elephants.

Elephants love water, so getting a shower and scrub is one of their favourite parts of the day.

10:30am Tea break. The keepers have a break and talk elephants!

11.00am We spend two hours deep-cleaning the entire elephant barn. It's back-breaking work (have you seen how much poo an elephant produces?) – but only the best will do for our herd!

1.00pm Lunchtime for the keepers. We have a dining room in the elephant barn, so we're never far away from them. The walls are covered with our favourite elephant photos and newspaper stories.

The elephants at ZSL Whipsnade Zoo play in their paddock.

A keeper helps a baby elephant learn to lift his foot.

At ZSL Whipsnade the public can get a close look at the elephants when they go for their daily walk.

ELEPHANTASTIC!
At ZSL Whipsnade Zoo's Elephantastic! demonstrations, elephants and their keepers display their elephant training methods. Elephants show off skills like lifting their feet to be cleaned, lying down on command, or carrying branches with their trunks.

2.00pm After lunch we take the herd for a walk around the zoo, every day, come rain or shine. In summer, we finish it with the Elephantastic! demonstration. In winter, the herd get some extra time to munch on trees – to the dismay of the gardeners!

4.00pm Back at the barn, the elephants are given their dinner.

8.00pm One or two keepers come back to check the elephants and give them some supper. We always say goodnight to them too!

ELEPHANT CALVES

There are few animals cuter than a baby elephant.
But although they're cute, they're not that small.
Even a newborn elephant weighs about 100kg –
more than most humans – and stands up to 1m tall.

Meeting and mating

Male and female elephants usually live separately, in their own herds.
But to mate, a male and a female have to get together. They find each other by their **scent**, and by making loud mating calls. Young elephants take an unusually long time to grow into adults. They are finally ready to **breed** (have babies) when they are about 13 or 14.

This African elephant calf has started to grow its adult tusks.

BABY TUSKS

Just like us, baby elephants are born with "milk teeth". Their proper tusks only start to grow after the tiny "milk tusks" have fallen out, when the elephant is about two years old.

Having a baby

Elephants are also pregnant for longer than other animals. It takes almost two years for an elephant calf to grow inside its mother's body. When it is born, it feeds on its mother's milk, like other **mammals** such as dogs and humans.

There is almost always just one baby. Elephants do very occasionally have twins. But if this happens in the wild, usually only one of them survives, as the mother does not normally have enough milk for two.

FACT FILE:
HOW ELEPHANTS GROW UP

0-6 months: Feeds only on milk
6 months: Starts eating plants
5-10 years old: Stops feeding on milk.
13 or 14: Young male elephants leave the herd, while females stay and have their own calves or help to look after baby brothers or sisters.
Elephant lifespan: up to 70 years

When a calf is born, its trunk is small and not very strong.

NAMING GEORGE

In April 2010, Karishma, an Asian elephant at ZSL Whipsnade Zoo, gave birth to a new baby boy elephant. To raise money for elephant conservation, an auction was held to name the calf. The person who offered the most money was allowed to name him, and called him George.

Baby Asian elephant George shelters close to his mum, Karishma.

ONE ELEPHANT'S STORY: AZIZAH

Azizah is a female Asian elephant living at ZSL Whipsnade Zoo. She's had an eventful life, and has travelled halfway around the world to get to where she is today.

Born in the wild

Azizah was born a wild elephant in the forests of Malaysia, southeast Asia, in 1984. Unfortunately, as Azizah and her mother roamed around looking for food, they began to raid local farms for crops. They caused so much damage that they had to be moved.

When this happened, Azizah became separated from her mother, and was taken to Malaysia's Malaka Zoo. There she was known as Layang Layang, the name of a Malaysian island. She was hand-reared by the keepers, who fed her milk from a bottle.

This is the kind of wild forest habitat where Azizah was born, in her homeland of Thailand.

WHAT IS AZIZAH LIKE?

Azizah is usually a very calm elephant – but she has a tendency for star-gazing and is often found daydreaming. Her keepers think she's probably a genius elephant, and is pondering the wonders of the universe!

Azizah's journey

When she was two years old, the Malaysian government gave Layang Layang to ZSL London Zoo as a gift. In London, she got her new name, Azizah. For the next year, she continued to be bottle-fed. She settled in well at ZSL London Zoo, but in 2001, it was time to move home again! All of the elephants in London were moved to ZSL Whipsnade Zoo, which is a lot more spacious and better suited to large roaming animals like elephants.

Becoming a mum

Since then, Azizah has been an integral part of Whipsnade's elephant herd, and she has turned out to be a great breeder. She has had three calves: Euan, born in 2004, Donaldson, born in 2008, and her new baby, born in 2011.

Azizah with her herd, enjoying the autumn leaves at Whipsnade.

Azizah stands protectively over her tiny calf who was born in October 2011, after a pregnancy that lasted 700 days!

THREATS TO ELEPHANTS

These are some of the things that reduced numbers of elephants in the past, and can make it hard for them to survive today.

Elephant hunting

Long ago, people could hunt "big game" (large wild animals) as much as they liked. Many hunters took pride in killing the biggest animals they could – such as elephants! The elephants were then stuffed, or made into objects such as elephant's foot waste-paper bins.

An old illustration of a hunter taking aim at a herd of African elephants.

Elephant products

People also hunted elephants for their meat, skin, and ivory – the bone from the tusks. It was once used to make ornaments, knife and fork handles, piano keys, musical instruments, buttons and many other things. Ivory became less popular in the 1900s, when plastic was invented, and when people realised that using it harmed elephants. But some people still want it, so hunters still **poach** elephants – which means they hunt them even though it's against the law.

A bin made of an elephant's foot was a desirable household item in Victorian times.

ARE ELEPHANTS REALLY DANGEROUS?

Elephants are often seen as wise, calm, peaceful creatures. But an angry elephant can be seriously deadly, especially a male in musth, or a female who is protecting a calf. Elephants kill many people each year by trampling them or **goring** them with their tusks. This is one reason people who live near elephants sometimes try to get rid of them.

A big elephant charging towards you is a scary sight – and very dangerous!

Size matters

Because they are so big, elephants need a lot of space and food. If villages and farms start to take over their habitat, elephants end up competing for these things with humans. Being so big and strong, they can be deadly enemies. So people kill them to protect themselves, their homes and their crops.

Bits and pieces

Another problem is that roads, farms and villages break elephant habitat up into small areas. This is called **habitat fragmentation**. It means elephants can't roam around freely to find food, water or a mate.

WHAT ARE TUSKS?

Elephants' tusks are front teeth that grow incredibly long and strong. Elephants use them to dig for roots, chip bark off trees, and fight their enemies. Ivory made from tusks is very strong.

You can see these African elephants' tusks clearly as they play in a mud bath.

HELPING THE ELEPHANTS

Trying to help wild elephants is a tricky job. Local people aren't always keen to protect them, because they are dangerous and can cause damage. Working with elephants can be risky for scientists and conservation workers too. And for some poor people, poaching elephants might be the only way to make a living. But there are things we can do!

Saving habitats

Governments can make laws to ban logging, farming and building in wild elephant habitat, to save it from being destroyed.

A safe place to live

Elephants can live more safely in **national parks** and **wildlife reserves**, special protected areas that have wardens to guard the animals and catch poachers.

Stopping poaching

As well as banning elephant hunting, a worldwide ban on trading ivory has been agreed, so it is illegal to buy or sell it. Occasionally some **confiscated** ivory is still sold to raise money for conservation.

A pile of African elephant tusks, ready to be sold for ivory.

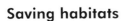

Tourists get close to a wild elephant on a safari trip.

Elephant attractions

One way to help endangered species is to make money from them being alive, instead of dead! National parks can become **ecotourism** attractions, where visitors pay to come and see elephants and other wildlife.

These tourists are being taken for an elephant ride, on trained Asian elephants.

This sign in Sri Lanka warns motorists to watch out for elephants, allowing them to move around more safely.

New jobs

Money from tourists pays local people to work as park managers, wardens or wildlife tour guides. Conservation schemes can also give local people jobs. This means there are fewer people logging, farming or poaching for a living.

Living together

Some conservation projects help people to live alongside elephants. They find ways to protect homes and crops, and give the elephants safe routes through their ranges.

Finding out more

Scientists need to find out as much as they can about elephants. The more we know, the easier it is to help elephants by protecting the right areas, and giving them the things they need most.

ELEPHANT STUDIES

We only know as much as we do about elephants because scientists have studied them carefully. They've tracked them in the wild, watched them closely in zoos, and even looked at elephants' insides. But there's still a lot more for them to find out.

Where are they?

To help elephants, we need to know where they live, how many of them there are, and how much space they use. Then we can pinpoint the best places to protect. Elephants aren't always easy to find, especially ones that live in forests. But scientists and researchers have other ways to **monitor** them, or keep track of them, such as counting their footprints and dung heaps, and the marks they leave on trees.

These elephants are gathering to suck water out of a hole they've found in the ground.

What are they doing?

Besides watching and counting elephants, scientists study what they get up to. They keep track of where, when and how elephants **raid** crops or villages, making maps of their movements. They can then work out the best places to put fences, or grow the most elephant-proof crops. They can even identify a particular elephant that is causing trouble. One solution for particularly troublesome elephants is to fit them with a radio collar that sends a text message to farmers when they get near to their fields.

Elephant-spotting

To get a good view of elephants, scientists sometimes wait near a lake or river, and count the elephants as they come to drink. In grassland areas, scientists spot elephants from the air, using a small aeroplane, **microlight** or hot air balloon.

In grasslands, such as this grassy plain in Kenya, Africa, elephants are easier to spot.

A fresh pile of elephant poo on a road in Zimbabwe, Africa.

WHOSE POO?

Working in zoos, scientists have found ways to tell from an elephant's droppings whether it's a female, and whether she is pregnant or could become pregnant. In the wild, they can use this to find out much more about wild elephants in an area, even without seeing them.

THE SALAK PRA PROJECT

Salak Pra is a wildlife sanctuary in Thailand, where around 150 Asian elephants live. ZSL helps to run a project there to find ways for the elephants to live safely side by side with farmers and villagers.

A wild place

Salak Pra is made up of wild forest habitat, but it is almost cut off from other wild areas by farms, towns and roads. The elephants naturally try to wander over a wider area, and sometimes raid nearby farms and villages for food. A large herd of elephants can munch up a whole field of maize or bananas in a few hours. Elephants have also been known to kill people, and people have killed them in revenge.

Maps and measurements

First of all, the conservation workers monitor the elephants' activities. They keep records of which fields and villages they visit, at what times of the year. They make maps of crop-raiding hotspots, and work out where the elephants are most likely to go at any one time. With this information, they can decide where to take action.

Elephants can cause a lot of damage to crops, even when they don't mean to. This coriander crop has been crushed by huge elephant feet.

Elephant repellents

Over time, studies at Salak Pra have found several safe ways to keep elephants away from precious crops:

- Watchtowers or platforms built high in trees let people look out for elephants, and scare them away before they can get into the fields.
- Elephants hate loud noises, so using a firecracker to make a loud bang scares them off.
- CDs hanging on strings, next to a lit torch, make a flashing effect that frightens elephants.
- Electric fences can work, but are expensive. Some farmers make fake electric fences that look like the real thing to the elephants.
- Farmers tie ropes around their fields and spread them with a stinky mixture of engine oil, chilli and tobacco. Elephants hate the smell.
- Switching to crops elephants don't like to eat, such as chilli plants and rubber trees, is a good way to get rid of them!

A farmer takes a turn on a lookout platform, watching out for elephants.

Shiny CDs, dangling in the breeze around a crop field, reflect flashes of light to scare elephants away.

ELEPHANT-SAVING SCHEMES

Lots of wildlife organisations are at work to help elephants. There are large and small schemes, in all the countries where elephants can be found.

African forest elephants

Like Asian elephants, African forest elephants live mainly in the jungle, where they can be hard to spot. Organisations are monitoring forest elephants in central Africa to find out how many there are and where they live.

Some areas of the forest elephant's habitat are destined to be cut down for timber. ZSL's Wildlife Wood project helps timber companies to do this without disturbing the elephants too much. They also leave some areas of wild forest for the wildlife, with smaller strips of forest, or **wildlife corridors**, linking them together.

An African forest elephant chews a mouthful of grass in its wild home.

HELPING THE FOREST

African forest elephants help the forest **ecosystem** – the habitat and other living things in it. They spread seeds around, bring down trees and fruits that other animals feed on, and make pathways that other animals use.

Finding hidden elephants

Conservation group Fauna &
Flora International runs Asian
elephant schemes in Cambodia,
Indonesia and several other
countries. They are studying
remote, mysterious areas, such as
the Dalai Plateau in Cambodia,
to see if elephants live there.

Asian elephants often live
deep inside thick forests,
like this one in Thailand.

Elephant crossing

In some parts of India, elephants
are often killed on roads, or by trains
or electric power lines, as they try
to move between different parts of
their range. A wildlife charity called
Elephant Family runs a project to
create safe wildlife corridors to help
them stay safe.

TOO MANY ELEPHANTS!

In Africa, schemes to help
elephants, such as banning ivory
hunting and setting up protected
reserves, can have good results.
In some places in East and
Southern Africa, elephants are
surviving and breeding so well
that there are too many of them.
They have to be caught and
moved to other areas.

This sign in Thailand is warning
people to watch out for
elephants crossing the road.

ELEPHANT ENCOUNTER: TWINKLE TOES

The staff at Salak Pra in Thailand don't often see the elephants, as they are shy and hide in the forest. As elephants can be dangerous, it's not sensible to get too close. But sometimes, they do spot signs, such as footprints, that show an elephant has been close by. One example was an elephant the workers nicknamed Twinkle Toes, because he was so careful where he put his feet!

Baby trees

One of the projects in the area is a tree nursery, where villagers grow young trees until they are big enough to be planted in the forest. The aim is to repair damaged parts of the forest, making more habitats for wildlife. The tree nursery is right next to the forest.

An Asian elephant this size has to be incredibly careful to tiptoe around a plant nursery, without knocking anything over.

These footprints show where Twinkle Toes has been. Luckily, he didn't damage any trees.

Twinkle Toes breaks in!

One night, the electric fence surrounding the protected forest area broke down. So one of the elephants took his chance to go for a wander into uncharted territory. His footprints showed that he tiptoed into the tree nursery for a nose around, and wandered over to look at some tree saplings. Then he did a graceful three-point-turn, and ambled back to the forest.

All in order

When the nursery staff found the elephant's trail, they were amazed that he hadn't done more damage. Elephants are well-known for tearing down trees and smashing their way around – but Twinkle Toes was incredibly gentle and careful. It was lucky he was, too. He could easily have destroyed the whole nursery, which would have cost a lot of money to replace.

"I COULDN'T BELIEVE IT!"

Belinda Stewart-Cox, who runs the project at Salak Pra, said: "This elephant appears to have been deliberately careful not to damage anything. He lifted the back fencepost and laid it down, before making his way down an aisle of tree saplings only three feet wide. I was absolutely astonished."

Belinda Stewart-Cox, who works for ZSL with elephants in Thailand.

ELEPHANTS AT NIGHT

Elephants are active in the daytime, but they often go exploring or looking for food at night too – especially if there are humans around who they would rather avoid. Another elephant at Salak Pra, nicknamed Polite Tusker, sometimes wanders through the office buildings at night – also without causing any damage.

Even if an elephant is *very* quiet, signs like these can reveal where he's been!

SEE ELEPHANTS YOURSELF

For centuries, elephants have been used as a spectacle to draw crowds and make money. If they are poorly looked after, or treated with cruelty, they can suffer horribly. But it doesn't have to be like that! There are ways for you to see and admire happy elephants, while making sure your money is used to help them.

On safari

A safari used to mean a trip to Africa to hunt wild animals. Today, it means a trip to *watch* wild animals and take photos, not to harm them. You can go on a whole safari holiday, or just take a day trip, usually to a national park, where expert guides show you where and how to watch the wildlife safely.

Elephant sanctuaries

In many Asian countries like India, Thailand, Laos and Sri Lanka, there are elephant sanctuaries to care for retired, injured or orphaned elephants. They make money to care for the elephants by charging tourists to visit. Sometimes you can even feed them or watch them have a bath.

These tourists on safari are getting a great view of elephants at a watering hole.

Volunteering

Lots of elephant sanctuaries and national parks have schemes for **volunteers** to work at them for a couple of weeks, or even a few months. The volunteers pay for their visit, and help with jobs like cleaning up after the elephants, counting them or working in the park offices.

Baby Asian elephants at a sanctuary in Thailand get a snack of bananas!

AN ELEPHANT ENCOUNTER

Some zoos, including ZSL's London and Whipsnade, hold special sessions where you can meet elephants up close, or even spend a day as a zookeeper.

Camera crews and TV presenters often make documentaries in national parks, where they can get close to wildlife fairly safely.

A worker takes an elephant for a bath at an elephant orphanage in Malaysia.

GO TO THE ZOO

Seeing elephants in the wild might involve a big, expensive trip. If you don't want to go that far, you might be able to see real elephants at a zoo or wildlife park near where you live. (Check first, though, as not all zoos have elephants.) Some places to visit are listed on page 46.

CONSERVATION BREEDING

Conservation breeding **means helping animals in captivity, such as in a zoo,** to have babies. It can be a good way to help an endangered species increase in number. But does it work for elephants?

Breeding problems

Most elephants living in zoos are female, because male elephants are hard to look after. It's also hard work to move big bull elephants from one place to another, to match them up with females to breed.

On top of this, while some animals are good at breeding in captivity, elephants sometimes seem to find it harder to get pregnant.

DID YOU KNOW?

Most animals live longer in zoos than in the wild, because they are protected from natural predators. But many zoo elephants seem to have shorter lives than wild ones. This could change, now that most zoo elephants have much bigger and better enclosures.

These male and female African zoo elephants are getting ready to mate.

This **ultrasound scan** shows another baby, George, growing inside his mother. Scans like these tell keepers if the unborn baby is healthy.

In this photo, Euan is still a calf, but getting quite big and grown-up!

Can it be fixed?

No one knows exactly why elephants don't always breed as well in captivity as they do in the wild. Bigger, more open and natural-style enclosures are becoming more common, and this could help. Some zoos, such a ZSL Whipsnade Zoo, have had great success breeding Asian elephants.

Success story

Euan, an Asian elephant calf, was born in captivity at ZSL Whipsnade Zoo in 2004. As he would in the wild, he stayed with his mother, Azizah, and his herd for some years. In 2011, he was moved to La Reserva animal reserve in Seville, Spain. There, he might one day be able to breed.

ELEPHANTS ON FILE

Zoos that keep elephants work together to make a **studbook**, a list of all the elephants in captivity, who is related to who, and which couples have mated and had calves. This helps them plan which elephants to move and put into pairs. The studbook for Asian elephants in Europe is held at Rotterdam Zoo in the Netherlands.

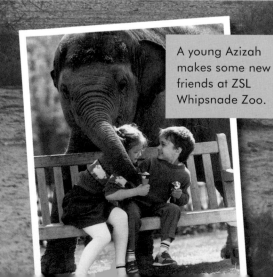

A young Azizah makes some new friends at ZSL Whipsnade Zoo.

CAN WE SAVE THE ELEPHANT?

Will Asian elephants, or other types of elephants, become extinct? It's hard to be sure. The problems that threaten them have not gone away. There is still a lot of work that needs to be done to help them.

Stopping the slide

In some ways, the efforts we've made to help elephants have worked. As recently as the 1980s, all types of elephants were disappearing fast. Today, thanks to poaching laws, national parks and reserves, and conservation schemes, African savannah elephants are starting to recover. Maybe, with the right help, African forest elephants and Asian elephants will too.

People like elephants

Compared to some endangered animals, like toads, spiders or bats, elephants are quite lucky, because they are very popular. In many countries, attitudes have changed and now no one wants to buy ivory or other elephant parts.

People feel concern, respect and awe towards elephants. We love to see them in zoos, in national parks, and in the wild - but not in circuses and shows where they might be mistreated. Because of their popularity, people will pay to visit elephants and support elephant conservation.

There's no need to make piano keys from ivory - other materials work just as well.

Top of the heap

Luckily for elephants, they are usually not on the menu for other animals. When animals are endangered, being eaten by tigers, wolves or other predators can be the last straw. This doesn't happen to fully-grown elephants, as they are bigger than these predators, and more than a match for them. The biggest threat to adult elephants is actually humans.

Elephants used to be a common sight in the circus – today they are used much less.

HOW CAN YOU HELP?

- Visit elephants at the zoo – you'll learn more about them, and your fee will be used to help them.
- You, your family or your class could adopt an elephant.
- Go elephant-watching if you're on holiday where elephants live.

At Whipsnade and many other zoos, you could visit beautiful elephants like Karishma and her calf George, shown here.

ABOUT ZSL

The Zoological Society of London (ZSL) is a charity that provides conservation support for animals both in the UK and worldwide. We also run ZSL London Zoo and ZSL Whipsnade Zoo.

Our work in the wild extends to Asia, where our conservationists and scientists are working to protect elephants from extinction. These awe-inspiring animals are part of ZSL's EDGE of Existence programme, which is specially designed to focus on genetically distinct animals that are struggling for survival.

By buying this book, you have helped us raise money to continue our conservation work with elephants and other animals in need of protection. Thank you.

To find out more about ZSL and how you can become further involved with our work visit **zsl.org** and **zsl.org/edge**

African savannah elephants are currently surviving better in the wild than their Asian cousins.

ZSL
LIVING CONSERVATION

EDGE

ZSL
LONDON
ZOO

ZSL
WHIPSNADE
ZOO

Websites

Asian elephant at ZSL Whipsnade Zoo
www.zsl.org/elephants

Asian elephant at EDGE of Existence
www.zsl.org/edge

Adopt an elephant
www.zsl.org/adoptelephant

ZSL information on African forest
elephants
**www.zsl.org/conservation/
regions/africa/forest-elephant**

Elephant Conservation Network
www.ecn-thailand.org

Places to visit

ZSL Whipsnade Zoo
Dunstable, Bedfordshire, LU6 2LF, UK
www.zsl.org/whipsnade
0844 225 1826

Baby elephants are the key to future population growth, so helping elephants to breed is vital.

Elephants are happiest when they have plenty of space to roam and explore.

GLOSSARY

aggressive Easily annoyed or violent.

breed Mate and have babies.

browse Leafy branches used as food for animals.

bull A male elephant.

calf A baby elephant.

captivity Being kept in a zoo, wildlife park or garden.

confiscated To have something taken away by the authorities.

conservation Protecting nature and wildlife.

conservation breeding Breeding animals in zoos.

cow A female elephant.

dung Elephant poo.

ecosystem A habitat and the living things that are found in it.

ecotourism Visiting wild places as a tourist to see wildlife.

EDGE Short for Evolutionarily Distinct and Globally Endangered.

enclosure A secure pen, cage or other home or for a zoo animal.

endangered At risk of dying out and become extinct.

extinction To no longer exist as a species.

fertilizer Something that makes soil better for growing plants.

gore To stab with horns or tusks.

GPS Short for Global Positioning System, a way of finding where you are.

habitat The natural surroundings that a species lives in.

habitat fragmentation Breaking up natural habitat into small areas.

habitat loss Damaging or destroying habitat.

herbivore pellets Special food for pet or zoo herbivores, or plant-eaters.

IUCN Short for the International Union for Conservation of Nature.

ivory Material made from elephants' tusks, or other animal teeth.

logging Cutting down trees.

mahout Someone who looks after and trains an elephant.

mammal A kind of animal that feeds its babies on milk from its body.

microlight A very small, light aircraft.

monitor To check, measure or keep track of something.

musth A bad-tempered, violent state that male elephants go into.

national park A protected area of land where wildlife can live safely.

poaching Hunting animals that are protected by law and shouldn't be hunted.

population Number of people, or animals, in a particular place.

predator An animal that hunts and eats other animals.

raid To attack or steal.

range The area where an animal or species lives.

rare Very few and far between.

satellite An object orbiting the planet.

scent A special smell.

scrub A dry landscape with small, tough plants.

shoot The first growth of a plant from a seed.

sociable Friendly and happy to be with others.

species A particular type of living thing.

stampede Lots of animals running at once.

studbook A record of the animals of a particular species born in captivity.

subspecies A slightly different type of animal from the main species.

ultrasound scan A way of using sound waves to look inside the body.

vibrations Shaking movements.

volunteer Someone who offers to do a job without being paid.

vulnerable At risk, but not as seriously as an endangered species.

watering hole A pool where animals come to drink.

wildlife corridor A strip of natural habitat connecting wild areas.

wildlife reserve A protected area of land where wildlife can live safely.

ZSL Short for Zoological Society of London.

FIND OUT MORE

Books

Elephants Under Pressure by Kathy Allen, Fact Finders, 2010

100 Things You Should Know About Elephants by Camilla de la Bedoyere, Miles Kelly Publishing, 2007

The Elephant Scientist by Caitlin O'Connell, Houghton Mifflin Harcourt, 2011

Who Scoops Elephant Poo? Working at a Zoo by Margie Markarian, Raintree, 2010

What's it Like to be a... Zoo Keeper? by Elizabeth Dowen and Lisa Thompson, A&C Black 2010

Websites

Asian elephants at Chester Zoo
www.chesterzoo.org/animals/mammals/Elephants/asian-elephants

BBC Asian elephant information, videos and sounds
www.bbc.co.uk/nature/life/Asian_Elephant

Elephant webcams
www.animalcameras.com/elephants/live-elephant-webcams/

Places to visit

Chester Zoo
Upton-by-Chester,
Chester CH2 1LH, UK
www.chesterzoo.org
01244 380280

Twycross Zoo
Burton Road, Atherstone,
Warwickshire CV9 3PX, UK
www.twycrosszoo.org

Smithsonian National Zoo
3001 Connecticut Avenue NW,
Washington, DC 20008, USA
http://nationalzoo.si.edu/

San Diego Zoo
2920 Zoo Drive, Balboa Park,
San Diego, California, USA
www.sandiegozoo.org

Rotterdam Zoo
Blijdorplaan 8, 3041 JE Rotterdam,
The Netherlands
www.rotterdamzoo.nl

INDEX

OTHER TITLES IN THE ANIMALS ON THE EDGE SERIES

www.storiesfromthezoo.com

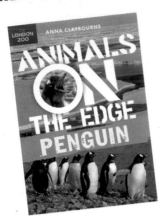

Penguin
ISBN: HB 978-1-4081-4822-8
PB 978-1-4081-4960-7

Rhino
ISBN: HB 978-1-4081-4823-5
PB 978-1-4081-4956-0

Tiger
ISBN: HB 978-1-4081-4824-2
PB 978-1-4081-4957-7

Gorilla
ISBN: HB 978-1-4081-4825-9
PB 978-1-4081-4959-1

Hippo
ISBN: HB 978-1-4081-4826-6
PB 978-1-4081-4961-4